A Kiss Like This

x ♡ x

Catherine and Laurence Anholt

F

FRANCES LINCOLN
CHILDREN'S BOOKS

When Little Cub was born,
Big Golden Lion just
couldn't stop kissing him.

"*GRRR!*" he growled.
"You're the most kissable cub
in the world."

Big Golden Lion kissed Little Cub behind his prickly ears . . .

just like this.

And Little Cub giggled.

He kissed Little Cub on the end of his small pink nose . . .

just like this.

And Little Cub wriggled.

He kissed Little Cub right on his warm fat tummy
and blew a raspberry on his belly button . . .

just like this.
x♥x

And Little Cub giggled and wriggled and jiggled.

In the golden evening sunshine,
Little Cub played outside.

Everyone who passed by and saw Little Cub wanted to kiss him too.

They just couldn't help it.

Along came Jumpy Monkey

and gave Little Cub
a tickly monkey kiss
behind his prickly ears,

on the end of his small pink nose

and right in the middle
of his warm fat tummy . . .

just like this.

And Little Cub giggled and wriggled and jiggled.

Along came Squawky Parrot

and gave Little Cub
a pecky parrot kiss behind
his prickly ears,

on the end of
his small pink nose

and right in the middle of his warm fat tummy . . .

just like this.

And Little Cub giggled and wriggled
and jiggled even more.

Along came Big Fat Rhino

and gave Little Cub
a nuzzling nosy rhino kiss
behind his prickly ears,

on the end of
his small
pink nose

and right in the middle of his warm fat tummy . . .

just like this.

And Little Cub giggled and wriggled
and jiggled all over again.

Along came Slippery Snake

and gave Little Cub a
s-s-slow hiss-s-sing
s-s-snake kiss-s-s behind
his prickly ears-s-s,

on the end
of his small
pink nos-s-se

and right in the middle of his warm fat tummy

just like this-s-s. x♡x

And Little Cub giggled and wriggled
and jiggled even more still.

Along came Old Grey Elephant

and gave Little Cub
a slurpy sloppy elephant kiss
behind his prickly ears,

on the end of
his small pink nose

and right in the middle of his warm fat tummy . . .

just like this.

And Little Cub giggled and wriggled
and jiggled more than ever.

Then, last of all, along came
Mean Green Hungry Crocodile
snapping his wicked white teeth.

He saw Little Cub
playing in the golden
evening sunshine.

"Little Cub, you certainly
are the most kissable cub
in the world.

"Come over here
and I will give you
a snippy snappy crocodile kiss."

But Little Cub didn't want a snippy
snappy crocodile kiss at all.

And he began to cry.

Mean Green Hungry Crocodile opened
his mean green hungry mouth and showed
all his wicked crocodile teeth . . .

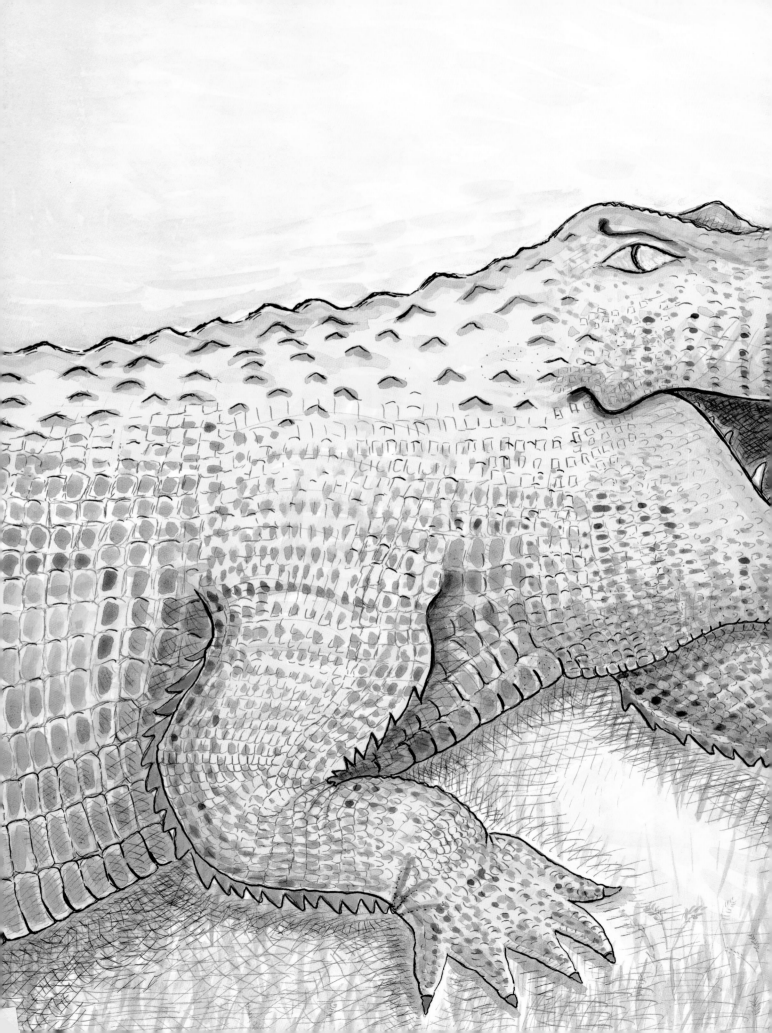

Quick as a flash, along came
Big Golden Lion and *roared*
            a Big Golden Lion ROAR
until Mean Green Hungry Crocodile turned and ran away.

Big Golden Lion carried Little Cub
back to their safe warm home and
tucked him into his safe warm bed.

Then Big Golden Lion
stretched himself.
"Listen, Little Cub," he said.

"There's nothing better
than a tickly monkey kiss –
when you're a tiny monkey.

"And a parrot peck is perfect –
when you're a baby parrot.

"No one loves a rhino
nuzzle quite like
a newborn rhino.

"A s-s-snake kiss-s-s is especially nic-c-ce when you're a baby snake.

"And you can't have too many elephant kisses — when you're a little elephant.

"And **even** snippy snappy baby crocodiles love snippy snappy kisses."

"But," said Big Golden Lion, yawning,
"when you're a sleepy Little Lion Cub,
there's only one thing in the whole wide world
that's completely, exactly right . . .

"And that's . . ."

A HUGE GREAT
Big Golden Lion kiss . . .

just like this!

*For Jill Anholt with
a kiss like this* x♡x

Visit the Anholt website at www.anholt.co.uk

A Kiss Like This copyright © Frances Lincoln Limited 2008
Text copyright © Laurence Anholt 2008
Illustrations copyright © Catherine Anholt 2008

The right of Laurence Anholt to be identified as the Author
and Catherine Anholt to be identified as the Illustrator
of this work has been asserted by them in accordance
with the Copyright, Designs and Patents Act, 1988.

First published in Great Britain in 1997 by Hamish Hamilton Limited,
a division of the Penguin Group.
This edition published in Great Britain in 2008 and in the USA in 2009
by Frances Lincoln Limited, 4 Torriano Mews, Torriano Avenue, London NW5 2RZ

British Library Cataloguing in Publication Data available on request

ISBN 978-1-84507-862-1

Set in Joanna

Printed in China

1 3 5 7 9 10 8 6 4 2